ADULT SKILLS Literacy for Living

Reading Comprehension – Book 3

Edited by Dr Nancy Mills and Dr Graham Lawler

The Adult Skills Range

The range of Adult Skills resources has been developed by Aber Education in response to needs expressed by tutors, students and governmental agencies. The materials are appropriate for adults who require support in advancing their literacy and numeracy skills.

Dr Nancy Mills, Adult Literacy/Numeracy author and editor, has over 25 years of combined experience in the adult education areas of teaching, tutor training, developing curriculum resources and publishing. Dr Graham Lawler, Adult Literacy/Numeracy author and editor, has over 27 years of combined experience in the adult education areas of teaching, tutor training, developing curriculum resources and publishing.

Adult Reading Comprehension – Book 3

Ordering Code AS1002 • ISBN 978-1-84285-101-2

© 2009 Aber Publishing

P.O. Box 225,

Abergele

Conwy County LL18 9AY

Published in Europe by Aber Publishing. www.aber-publishing,co.uk

Cover illustration by Michelle Cooper

Contents

gr. 7-12 = 6 levels
30 pages
- every 5 is a gr. level. Approx.

© 2009 Aber Publishing – Adult Skills   Adult Reading Comprehension – Book 1

Introduction

Who is this resource for?

Reading Comprehension Book 3 includes 30 fiction and non-fiction short stories designed to provide reading and comprehension material at approximately years 7-12, higher than Reading Comprehension Books 1 and 2. Teens and adults who require literacy support are aware of their needs but often lack confidence in their reading ability and wish to improve and further develop their literacy skills. A significant result of their efforts in literacy programmes, in addition to increasing their reading skills, is the improvement of their self-image. They will be able to feel the effects in every part of their lives.

Adults who seek help may be motivated, by the desire to get a job, moving up the job ladder, or to gain independence in commonplace tasks such as sitting a driving exam, writing a grocery list, reading the newspaper or doing personal banking.

How is the resource organised?

The stories have been placed according to a continuum that gets gradually more difficult. They contain sentences that increase in length and vocabulary that increases in difficulty through the resource. Each story is accompanied with a relevant photo and five comprehension or research questions. You may ask students to do all or any one of them.

How is comprehension tested?

It doesn't matter whether they read every word correctly or whether they sound good when reading aloud. Understanding the meaning of the text, developing vocabulary and increasing their confidence are key outcomes.

Ask the students how you will know that they have understood the text. They will come to realise that by answering the questions accurately they are demonstrating that they have actually read the text and understood its meaning.

Questions test a variety of higher-level comprehension skills that require the reader to think beyond the words or to 'read between the lines', often picking up subtle clues that are not immediately obvious. These questions may require the reader to write answers based on their understanding or opinion of the story, draw conclusions, use context clues to make predictions, identify main ideas, identify parts of speech, do creative writing, complete grammar and vocabulary exercises, or use reference materials such as a dictionary, maps or the Internet.

Strategies

Analysis – encourage students to read analytically, thinking beyond the written information and relating what they read to their own experiences. Many questions can have more than one right answer, as long as the reasoning is logical.

Discussion – discuss what the story is about before asking them to read it or reading it to them.

Enrichment – students may find particular stories are more appealing than others. When they really enjoy a story, find related stories from other sources for them to read. These will be more likely to hold their interest and speed up their learning.

Photos/graphics – the photos with each story are selected to give context clues, something all readers do to assist us in understanding text.

Reading aloud – the way a student reads text aloud, and the way they emphasise and group words will give a good indication of their level of understanding. Readers need to learn to take risks without the fear of failure.

Repetition – students begin to recall words when reading text a second or third time. Developing skilled reading has a lot to do with reading 'mileage' – just doing the practice.

Revision – the stories can be effective when used for revision. Students may wish to re-read favourite stories a few months after their first reading.

Silent reading – silent reading is a highly developed ability which takes time to master. Help students gain confidence with this skill.

Word attack (decoding) – decoding skills must be taught so that students can apply them when reading independently.

Word identification – some words will be known by sight and reinforced in the text. For unknown words, adults have a wealth of experience which they can call upon. Teach them how to guess what a word means using the surrounding clues. Try using the word in a different context to reinforce its meaning. This skill will add to their self-confidence.

Photocopiable resources

The following is a list of some of the ways in which photocopiable resources, also called blackline masters or BLM, may be used in an instructional environment to ensure variety of presentation and moderation in photocopying costs.

- Copy the desired pages to A4 paper as needed. Students write on the sheet.

- Copy the resource to A4 paper at a rate of one sheet per group (two or more students). Students work together to complete one sheet between them.

- Copy all the pages required for the unit to form a booklet.

- Use peer tutoring by copying the resource for one student to use with another.

Ensure students understand the terms synonym and antonym before reading ' I thought I was going to die'.

© 2009 Aber Publishing – Adult Skills   Adult Reading Comprehension – Book 3

The Aboriginal Way

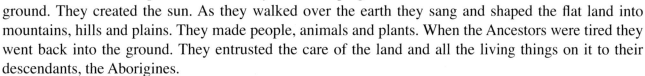

For the Australian Aborigines, the land is the source of life and meaning. Their view of the land stems from their perception of how the world was made. They believe that long ago the land was dark, flat, cold and barren. There was no sun. Nothing lived.

The Ancestors came up from where they were sleeping under the ground. They created the sun. As they walked over the earth they sang and shaped the flat land into mountains, hills and plains. They made people, animals and plants. When the Ancestors were tired they went back into the ground. They entrusted the care of the land and all the living things on it to their descendants, the Aborigines.

The places where the Ancestors went back into the ground are linked by the pathways that took the Ancestors on their various journeys. The Aborigines call these pathways the Dreaming Tracks and they call the time when the Ancestors were on the earth the Dreamtime.

The Aborigines still believe the spirits of the Ancestors live inside the earth and sky, and inhabit plants and animals. They also believe the Ancestors' spirits are always present in the land and the people.

Questions

1. What do Australian Aborigines believe is the source of life?

   _____

2. Define these words and use them in a sentence to show your understanding:

   ancestor   _____

   entrusted _____

   source   _____

3. Where do Australian Aborigines believe the ancestors came from?

   _____
   _____
   _____
   _____
   _____

4. List all of the plural words in this story. Don't repeat any words.

   _____   _____   _____   _____
   _____   _____   _____   _____
   _____   _____   _____   _____

5. Write a short summary of this story.

   _____
   _____
   _____

A Message from the Spirit World

Do you believe in ghosts? I didn't, but now I'm not sure. I had heard of mediums, mind readers, ESP, astral travel…but never thought that it would be something I'd be interested in.

Earlier this year I was invited to a theatre where a medium was going to be doing readings for people in the audience. When she appeared, the first thing she did was to explain that she sees spirits around her all the time no matter where she is - in the supermarket, at the airport, even at home. This is a natural part of her life.

As she began looking around the audience, her eyes focused on me. She said, "Who's Matthew?" I answered that Matthew was my father-in-law. She said, "He died suddenly of a heart attack." By then, she had my attention, because she was right on both accounts.

Next she described a woman 'with the initial G' who had pain in her arms, and asked if I knew who this was. I told her that it must be my favourite Auntie Gay who had debilitating arthritis in her forearms, wrists and hands for several years before she died. The medium informed me that my Auntie Gay was my spirit guide and was looking over me all the time.

For the next fifteen minutes she related accurate details about several other of my family members who had 'passed over'. Everything was spot on, as far as I knew.

Do we really go to a spirit world on 'the other side' after we die? Do we come back as spirits and see what's going on? Is it possible to get messages from the dead? What do you believe?

Questions

1. Answer the questions in the last paragraphs based on your beliefs.

   _____

   _____

2. Compare and contrast the following:

   medium   _____

   ESP   _____

   mind reader   _____

   psychic   _____

   astral travel _____

3. Is this story fact or opinion? Explain and support your answer.

   _____

   _____

4. Write two different definitions of these words - one of the definitions should be in the context of the story

   readings   _____   _____

   spirits   _____   _____

   accounts   _____   _____

   passed over _____   _____

5. Discuss any experiences you or your friends have had with the supernatural.

© 2009 Aber Publishing – Adult Skills   Adult Reading Comprehension – Book 3

I Thought I Was Going to Die

Last week my friends and I decided to go to a swimming hole we had heard about that was below a waterfall. We parked at the top of the falls, which were about 4 metres high. There was a well-worn track alongside them that we followed down to the pool. Heavy rain the night before meant that the water was more turbulent than normal, and also there was a huge amount of water spilling over the falls.

My mate Michael didn't want to swim, so he stayed on the side to be the lifeguard. He brought his camera so that he could document the outing. Everyone jumped in, and I dived down to touch the bottom but didn't succeed because it was much deeper than I expected. The whole time we were swimming, the falls seemed to be calling out to me - they looked so inviting. I swam over and treaded water right underneath them, feeling the power of the falling water on my head. Since I knew that the pool was so deep, I thought it would be safe to plunge over the falls and not hit the bottom.

When everyone saw me climbing up the track they tried to dissuade me from my plan. They were frightened for me but I was full of confidence and excitement. I got to the top and looked over, feeling like my heart was beating about 200 times a minute. Even though I was scared to death, I couldn't let on to my friends. What would they think?

Questions

1. Write a synonym and antonym for each of these words based on the meaning in the story.

   deep   _____   _____

   safe   _____   _____

   frightened   _____   _____

   friend   _____   _____

   heavy   _____   _____

   bottom   _____   _____

2. Explain what the author meant by 'the falls seemed to be calling out to me'.

   _____

   _____

3. Write two different definitions for these words. On the back of this page, write a sentence using each one as a noun and as a verb.

   document   _____   _____

   falls   _____   _____

   tread   _____   _____

   pool   _____   _____

4. Do you know how many times an average resting heart beats per minute and how many times it beats when doing rigorous exercise? Set up an experiment with people of different ages and sex and measure their heart rates during rest and exercise. Write a short report about your findings.

5. On a separate sheet of paper, write two different ending paragraphs for this story.

Our Place in Space

The universe contains billions of galaxies of different shapes and sizes. We are part of a galaxy called the Milky Way. A galaxy is an entire system of dust, gases and stars in space. Our sun is an ordinary star which lies about 30,000 light-years from the centre of the Milky Way. Each galaxy is made up millions of stellar systems. A stellar system is the orbit of planets around a star. The word solar means anything to do with the sun, so that is why we call our stellar system the solar system.

The sun is a huge ball of very hot gasses - up to 15 million degrees Celsius. Although it is 150 million kilometres away, the sun gives off energy that we receive as heat and light.

Our solar system is made up of nine planets and their moons. All the planets are orbiting the sun. The four planets which are the closest to the sun are Mercury, Venus, Earth and Mars. The next four planets are Jupiter, Saturn, Uranus and Neptune. Pluto was the ninth and furthest planet to be discovered in our solar system.

An interesting bit of trivia about Uranus is that its discoverer wanted to call it George. Wouldn't it have been strange to have a planet with that name?

Questions

1. Select a planet and write about some facts that astronomers have learned about it.

_____

_____

_____

_____

2. Write synonyms for these words from the story:

stellar	_____	orbit	_____	energy	
discovered	_____	centre	_____	closest	
trivia	_____	strange	_____	system	

3. Calculate the approximate temperature of the sun in degrees Fahrenheit.

4. How long is a light-year? _____

5. Do you believe there are intelligent beings on other planets in the universe? Support your opinion.

_____

_____

© 2009 Aber Publishing – Adult Skills   Adult Reading Comprehension – Book 3

The End of the Beach

Living near the beach is special in many ways. There is the continuous, hypnotising sound of the surf pounding on the sand. Seagulls, effortlessly soaring along the cliff top, constantly patrol the coast. The sunrise never ceases to delight, the colours displaying every imaginable shade of pink. The ever-changing cloud formations take on shapes and hues that stimulate the imagination.

Last weekend I walked along the shore as far as I could, to where the rocky cliffs jut out into the surf. There was a gentle breeze blowing toward me and before I got to the rocks I noticed a strong stench, which I couldn't identify. It soon became apparent that I was not alone when I heard a loud roar. A lone sea lion was perched on a rock and there was no doubt that she was aware of my presence. Just then, something caught my eye in the sea that looked like a piece of floating driftwood, getting tossed about by the swells. It was L-shaped like a broken branch, with a big bit in the water and a smaller bit protruding from the surface. An enormous roar broke my concentration and I looked away momentarily to ensure the seal was still on her rock. She was.

Searching again for the piece of driftwood, it wasn't to be seen. But when I looked once again at the sea lion on the rock, she had been joined by her small offspring, about the size of the piece of driftwood I had been studying. They were one and the same.

Questions

1. List five pairs of adjectives and nouns that go together in the story. Write a synonym for each of the adjectives.

    Adjective   Noun   Synonym

    _____   _____   _____

    _____   _____   _____

    _____   _____   _____

    _____   _____   _____

    _____   _____   _____

2. Explain the meaning of 'They were one and the same'.

    _____

    _____

3. Compare and contrast a sea lion and a seal.

    _____

    _____

4. On a separate sheet of paper, write a short poem about some part of nature that you enjoy. Use the dictionary to find some adjectives for the poem that describe your feelings.

5. What do you think was the author's purpose for using the image of driftwood to describe the baby seal?

    _____

© 2009 Aber Publishing – Adult Skills   Adult Reading Comprehension – Book 3

Not Just a Mushroom

What do you think of when you hear the word fungus? Most people think of mushrooms, toadstools and puffballs which can often be seen on our lawns, in paddocks and forests. Yeast, used in making bread and beer, is also a fungus.

We frequently come across other types of fungi in our everyday lives. Sometimes they are a nuisance to us - like mould on our fruit or mildew on our bread - but in nature they can be a tremendous advantage. To grow, fungi feed on organic material: living or dead plants and animals. As the fungi feed, they decompose the material into compost and therefore keep us literally from being buried in waste.

Another interesting fact about fungus is that it can cause disease and cure disease. Athlete's foot and ringworm are two common diseases in humans caused by fungi. Penicillin, the wonder drug of the 20th century, is a famous fungus that was discovered by accident. In 1928 a scientist named Alexander Fleming was trying to find ways of killing the bacteria that caused infection. He was doing an experiment when he noticed that a strange type of mould had prevented the growth of the bacteria he was working with. He didn't know it at the time, but he had discovered penicillin. With further experimentation he first determined that it was not poisonous, and then found that it prevented meningitis, diphtheria and pneumonia bacterium.

During World War I, people were alarmed by the number of soldiers who died of infection from their wounds. Luckily, Penicillin was discovered and mass-produced in time to save the lives of thousands of wounded soldiers in World War II.

Questions

1. Fungi do not produce flowers or seeds. Write about how it reproduces.

_____

_____

_____

2. Why was Penicillin called the 'wonder drug'?

_____

3. Explain the difference between: fungi and fungus; bacteria and bacterium.

_____

_____

4. List five different types of fungi and where you might find them.

_____

_____

_____

_____

_____

5. Are fungi edible or poisonous? Explain your answer and give examples.

_____

_____

_____

© 2009 Aber Publishing – Adult Skills   Adult Reading Comprehension – Book 3

The Story Behind Metals

People began using metals about 10,000 years ago. Copper, gold and silver, found in native rock deposits in the ground, were the first metals to be used.

Ore is rock that contains metal deposits. It is taken from the ground by opencast strip mining if it is near the surface (such as iron ore and aluminium ore). Underground mining is used for deep, below-the-surface deposits (such as copper and gold).

Some metals cannot be used in their pure form because they are generally too weak and soft. For example, mercury is a metal that becomes liquid at room temperature.

Metals can be enhanced by adding other metals to them. These combinations are called alloys. These mixtures may improve the strength and hardness of the metals. By mixing certain amounts of different metals, an alloy can be made which has ideal properties for a particular task. For example, nickel and chromium are added to steel to prevent it from rusting. This is called stainless steel.

Two other alloys are brass, which can be found in boat hardware and musical instruments; and pewter, which has been used to make mugs, plates, belt buckles and picture frames.

Questions

1. Which metal becomes liquid at room temperature? _____

2. Name three alloys not mentioned in the story and tell what they are used for.

   _____

   _____

   _____

3. Circle all the adjectives in the story. List six of them and give an antonym for each that can have more than one meaning. Write both meanings.

   _____   _____   _____

   _____   _____   _____

   _____   _____   _____

4. Write a short summary of this story.

   _____

   _____

   _____

   _____

   _____

5. What is the difference between opencast and underground mining?

   _____

   _____

   _____

   _____

© 2009 Aber Publishing – Adult Skills   Adult Reading Comprehension – Book 3

The Last Hunt

My brother and I were brought up on a farm in Wales where our father ensured that we were able to use firearms safely. Many hours were spent at target practice, where a friendly competition naturally occurred between my brother and me.

The first moving targets we learned to shoot were rats, adept at stealing from the animal food store, and rabbits, proficient at digging up newly planted vegetable gardens. Both were serious nuisances. Then we graduated to foxes, which would take the ducks and weak lambs. All of these were considered to be relentless pests.

The last time my brother and I went hunting was in the North Wales hills. We had decided to go on our first deer hunt one week in August. On the second day we saw a beautiful doe lurking in the forest amongst the trees. As we prepared for a shot, we were surprised when a small shape emerged from behind her. It was a brand new fawn, an unseasonal arrival since it was not yet spring. The fawn was timid and kept close to its mother, who was unaware of our presence as there was no breeze.

My brother and I looked at each other and knew that we were thinking the same thing. The rest of the week was spent hiking, reminiscing about our childhood memories by the fire at night, swimming in the river and enjoying each other's company. It was our last hunting trip.

Questions

1. Explain the title of the story.

    _____

    _____

    _____

2. Write synonyms for these words:
    reminisce _____   nuisance _____
    relentless _____   emerge _____

3. What is 'friendly competition'? Describe a situation where you have experienced this.

    _____

    _____

    _____

4. No matter how you feel, list three pros and three cons about hunting that could be used to debate the issue.

    _____

    _____

    _____

5. Research and describe methods that can be used to control pests, other than shooting them. Give one advantage and one disadvantage of each method.

    _____

    _____

    _____

How to Make a Mummy

Over 3000 years ago in Egyptian culture, it was generally believed that everyone went to an after-life when they died. The spirit of the dead person had to cross the River of the Dead to enter the Next World. A special ceremony was held to help this happen, but first the body had to be prepared.

Upon death the body was taken to an embalmer's workshop. Almost all the organs were removed, including the brain. With only the heart left inside, the body was treated with special oils, spices and perfumes. It was covered in a mixture of salt and soda which dried the body out.

After seventy days the body was wrapped in layers of linen bandages with amulets to protect the person on their journey to the Next World. The linen was coated with oil and resin. A mask, made of compressed paper and painted and decorated to look like the dead person, was placed over the head. Finally the body was placed in a wooden or plaster coffin. If the mummified body was a very important person, it was put in a decorated sarcophagus, or mummy case.

Objects that the dead person would need in the after-life were placed beside the body. The wealthy were buried with their own Book of the Dead that contained a map and various spells which would enable them to get through the gates to the Next World.

Questions

1. Why is Next World capitalised?_____

2. Give both synonyms and antonyms for these words:

   compressed   _____   _____

   preserve   _____   _____

   spirit   _____   _____

3. Do you believe in an after-life? Explain your belief.

   _____

   _____

   _____

   _____

4. What is an amulet? Why would the Egyptians believe that an amulet would protect them after death?

   _____

   _____

   _____

5. List six steps in the preparation of a body for mummification.

   _____

   _____

   _____

   _____

   _____

© 2009 Aber Publishing – Adult Skills   Adult Reading Comprehension – Book 3

A Welsh Rugby Mystery

Coaching rugby in Wales can have its trials, especially when the team is made up of stroppy eight to ten year olds. Each youngster has visions of playing for Wales, being too young to appreciate the unlikelihood of such an honour.

bad tempered

Taking advantage of their dreams, I assigned each team member the name of a present or past Wales player according to the position they were playing. We had Colin, Shane, Phil and Neil, as well as others. My wife wrote each name on sticky fabric which the players could temporarily put on their backs during practice. I suggested to them that during matches they try to visualise being the players whose names they borrowed.

By the end of the season, we had proven that visualisation could work. We won the South Wales regional championships by a landslide. For a surprise, I contacted an old friend of mine, a very famous Welsh national team player born in Cardiff, and invited him to come to our celebratory BBQ after the final match. I told the players that I had a surprise for them and that they should wear their Wales Rugby team names for the occasion.

When he arrived, the boys were so astonished they were speechless. You could hear a pin drop when he started praising the team for their great effort, and then he noticed the sticker on one of their backs. Laughing heartily, he had each of them turn around to display their names. This broke the ice, and for the rest of the evening he called them by their Wales team names. They all got his autograph. It was the most memorable after-match BBQ imaginable.

Questions

1. In the story, there are three pairs of words with similar meanings. Write each word and find its definition in the dictionary.

   _____   _____   _____

   _____   _____   _____

   _____   _____   _____

2. Name four positions on a rugby team. Next to each one, put the name of a famous Wales player who has played that position.

   _____   _____

   _____   _____

   _____   _____

   _____   _____

3. Who do you think was the surprise famous Wales player? Give your reasons for your answer.

   _____

4. Is this a believable story? Explain your answer.

   _____

   _____

5. What is your opinion about autographs? Why do people collect them? Do you think it is a worthwhile hobby? Explain your answer.

© 2009 Aber Publishing – Adult Skills   Adult Reading Comprehension – Book 3

Earth Movers

The Earth's crust is divided into six large and several smaller, rigid plates. Under the plates is the molten centre of the Earth. The jigsaw-like plates fit together but are continually moving and changing shape. Almost all seismic and volcanic activity can be attributed to plate movements. These movements are usually very slow - at about the same rate as it takes our fingernails to grow. The edges of these plates are called boundaries. There are three things that could be happening at a boundary between two plates. In one, molten rock rises to fill the gaps that are created as the boundaries move away from each other. This creates underwater valleys, trenches or volcanoes. The second type of movement is when the boundaries move together and collide, causing one plate to be pushed down underneath the other or forcing one plate upwards. This is how the Himalayas were formed. Volcanoes can also be formed in this way. A third possibility at a boundary is where the plates move parallel to each other in opposite directions, similar to cars on a road. Because the edges of the plates are jagged, the plates sometimes become locked together. When this happens, and enough pressure is exerted, the plates separate - often violently. This is the cause of most earthquakes.

Questions

1. Describe three types of movement at plate boundaries.

    _____

    _____

    _____

2. Research the major geographic features of the Earth that plate movements can create.

3. In the context of the story, explain the meaning of the words below. Then use each one in a sentence in a different context from that in the story.

    rigid _____

    _____

    locked _____

    _____

    violently _____

    _____

4. Learn about a major earthquake that has happened in the world. On a separate sheet, write a story about it.

5. Identify and list three keywords for each paragraph.

    _____   _____   _____

    _____   _____   _____

    _____   _____   _____

    _____   _____   _____

    _____   _____   _____

© 2009 Aber Publishing – Adult Skills   Adult Reading Comprehension – Book 3

The Cookie Monster

When I was young, I used to like to help my mother in the kitchen. I was probably more trouble than help, but that didn't worry me. I always knew when she was baking because of the aroma that filled the house. My favourite thing to do was to lick the bowl after she had made a cake or muffins - but cookies were my favourite.

One day after school, before Mum got home from work, it seemed to be time for me to take some real responsibility for the baking. I decided I would make cookies, and I chose the chocolate chip variety. Finding the recipe in my mother's tattered folder, I carefully read it through to ensure that all the ingredients were available before I commenced. Combining this, sifting that, blending this, folding in that… it was all quite a lot more complicated than I imagined. But that didn't impede me. In fact, full of confidence, I doubled the recipe to make 5 dozen.

Of course I had to taste the dough to ensure that the mixture would meet my mother's quality check when she got home. I determined that it did, and soon the cookie sheet was filled with row after row of dough blobs baking in the oven, about 30 in all. There was plenty left in the bowl - enough to do several more quality checks before the first ones were ready.

Unfortunately, only 30 cookies ever made it to the oven. The bowl well-licked, I cleaned up the kitchen to show I could complete the job. When Mum got home, she was totally puzzled about why I wasn't hungry for dinner or dessert.

Questions

1. Why do you think the writer decided that cookies would be the first item to bake? Explain your answer.

_____

_____

_____

2. What was meant when the author said she did 'several more quality checks'?

_____

_____

3. How many cookies is 5 dozen?   How much cookie dough did the author eat?

_____   _____

4. Find a recipe for something you would like to learn to make. Copy it, and then write it down again 'doubled'.

5. List the words in the story that refer to how ingredients are handled in a recipe and write their definitions from the dictionary. Find four additional words that are used in recipes to describe what to do with ingredients and give their dictionary definitions.

_____ _____ _____ _____

_____ _____ _____ _____

_____ _____ _____ _____

_____ _____ _____ _____

New Zealand's Haka

The haka is a unique display performed at the beginning of each All Black rugby match as well as by other New Zealand sports teams travelling in New Zealand and overseas. It is an expression of the enthusiasm, energy and competition felt by the players.

When was the haka first used in rugby? Tom Ellison was a member of the 1888 Native Team which toured New Zealand, Australia and Britain. He is credited with introducing the haka to rugby. He also designed the first All Black jersey as well as helping to develop the rules and New Zealand style of playing the game.

The word haka is the Maori word for dance. In the past, it was a Maori custom to welcome and entertain visitors with a haka. It was also used to tell the stories of what was happening in the lives of those performing it, to exhibit a protest or to depict important events. Sometimes the men had weapons in their hands while doing a haka.

Many people wonder about the meaning of the shaking of the hands during Maori hakas and dances. This movement symbolises the trembling of the air on hot summer days.

In the 2004 Olympics, the New Zealand Olympic team honoured medal winners returning to the Village with a haka.

Questions

1. When was the first rugby match played in New Zealand, who were the teams and who won?

   _____

   _____

   _____

2. Compare and contrast the Maori haka with the performance Tongan rugby players do before their matches.

   _____

   _____

3. List 6 verbs in this story. Give their present, past and future tense forms. For example: perform, performed, will perform

   _____ _____ _____
   _____ _____ _____
   _____ _____ _____
   _____ _____ _____
   _____ _____ _____
   _____ _____ _____

4. Think of another name for this story. _____

5. Have you ever seen a real-life a haka? If so, explain your feelings during the performance. If you have not ever done one, speak to someone who has and record his or her feelings.

   _____

Kamikazes in Fiji?

One of the most memorable experiences of my life was when I travelled to Fiji with my wife for our honeymoon. We didn't want to spend money on renting a car to get around the island, so we depended on the infamous bus service to transport us. The drivers can best be described as on schedule, and worst as kamikazes. In Fiji, these go hand in hand, as it's necessary to drive as quickly and recklessly as possible in order to arrive at a destination on time.

On our final day, we had to mentally prepare ourselves for a six-hour bus ordeal consisting of 21 starts and stops. The cost of the trip from Suva to Nadi was going to be £15 each. As we were waiting for the bus driver to appear, a taxi pulled up beside us. He was on his way back to Nadi after dropping off some customers and was hoping to find some fares to fill his car for the drive back.

"How much for two people?" we inquired, not expecting to be able to afford it.

"Forty pounds" he replied.

That was music to our ears. In we hopped, leaving him to sort out the luggage and pleased with ourselves for having such luck. No sooner did we think we were on our way than the driver pulled up to another couple waiting for the bus and offered them the same deal! As it turns out, they were also from the U.K.

The trip can both best and worst be described as close quarters because, even though five people in a taxi was a tight fit, we got to know the other couple really well and plan to catch up with them again some day in the U.K.

Questions

1. Write the definition of kamikaze as used in this story. Explain what the author means by it.

   _____

   _____

2. Locate Fiji on a map. Write the names of the two main islands, the capital city, and the name of the city where the international airport is. Do some research to discover two more facts about the country.

   _____   _____   _____

   _____

   _____

3. What does 'music to our ears' mean?

   _____

4. Write down three adverbs in this story. What do they have in common? _____
   Make two of them into adjectives.

   _____   _____

   _____   _____

   _____   _____

5. How much did the taxi driver make from the trip from Suva to Nadi? _____
   Do you think it was a good deal for the honeymooners? Explain your opinion.

   _____

   _____

The Kayapo Tribe

The Kayapo people are one of the five hundred different Amerindian tribes which live in the Amazon rainforest today. Kayapo villages have buildings made of wood with palm-leaf thatched roofs. The Kayapo people are totally self-sufficient.

The rainforest offers a great variety of food to eat. There are animals and birds to hunt, and fish to catch in the Xingu River and its streams. There are hundreds of different fruits to choose from in the forest, such as bananas and mangoes.

Every year women make gardens in forest clearings and plant crops like maize, sweet potatoes, pineapples, peppers, beans and yams. Special fertilisers are made out of plant leaves, ashes and termite nests. The Kayapo also collect honey from domestic, stingless bees.

Unfortunately, aspects of modern civilisation are finding their way into the Amazon forest and changing forever the way these tribal groups live. In time, the only way we will remember their lifestyle is through the notes, photographs and films of visitors.

Questions

1   You are a professional photographer and have been asked to photograph the Kayapo. However, you can only use 5 photos. Describe the 5 pictures you would take and explain why you chose them.

2   Do you think the Kayapo would be happier living a more modern lifestyle? Explain your answer.

3   Do you think that the Kayapo live a well-organised lifestyle? Why?

4   List pros and cons of living like the Kayapo.

5   Using reference materials, find and describe two other primitive civilisations that still exist.

This Old House

On my uncle and auntie's farm there is an old building that piques my curiosity each time we visit them. It is a decrepit old structure, but enough of it is still standing to give clues regarding how it might have appeared in its heyday.

It has a two-tier roofline that would have been a unique architectural design for the time. There was even a loft, with a homemade wooden staircase leading to it. No doubt the children clambered up there each night, where it would be snug and warm from the rising heat of the fire below. A big window at the front would have offered a cool breeze in the summer and a panoramic view of some of the paddocks. Three old mattresses can still be distinguished, although the rats have long since claimed them for themselves.

Downstairs was a small lounge and kitchen with a coal stove. Outside the kitchen, the lean-to would have furnished shelter for washing and a line for hanging out laundry on stormy days, providing protection from the rain.

The long drop was about 20 metres from the back door, and was faring much better than the house. Looking inside, we found that the seat had rotted away and the hole was filled in, but we could still distinguish ancient messages carved on the walls during lengthy sessions.

Across from the house is a huge tree with the remnants of a rope swing still visible on an upper limb. A wooden seat, or what is left of it, dangles from one end. It must have brought much joy to the children who grew up here.

Questions

1. The word *pique* has several meanings. Use a dictionary to find and write down as many of its definitions as you can find, and note whether each is a noun or verb.

   _____

   _____

   _____

2. Describe how the condition of the house compared to the long drop.

   _____

   _____

3. What does *heyday* mean? List two synonyms that the author could have used in its place.

   _____   _____   _____

4. Write a short poem about this house, using some of the words in the story, and give it a title.

   _____

   _____

   _____

   _____

5. Circle all the statements that are based on fact, and underline the statements that are based on opinion.

Adult Reading Comprehension – Book 3

Man in Space

Powered flight developed rapidly from the early 1900s. It was widely believed, up until the middle of the 20th Century, that human space flight was extremely unlikely. Many thought that landing humans on the moon was impossible.

During World War II, intensive work was done by Germans to develop rocket-powered bombs. These were known as 'buzz bombs' and were launched from France to bomb London. In one of the few positive outcomes of that war, a great deal of knowledge was gained about rocketry from Germany's experiments. After the war, some of the scientists involved in developing buzz bombs joined American and Soviet scientists to build rockets which could reach the outer atmosphere and beyond. In 1954, to the stunned amazement of the world, a Soviet rocket reached the outer atmosphere and launched the Sputnik satellite into orbit around the Earth. The race was on. Less than ten years later, in 1961, the first human flew into space. The first person set foot on the moon in 1969.

Today you can find few people who would totally dismiss the idea that man may, one day, visit another planet. Even the idea of travelling as fast or faster than the speed of light is considered by many to be remotely possible. After all, for many years it was doubted that travelling faster than the speed of sound was possible.

Questions

1. Compare and contrast powered and un-powered flight.

_____

_____

_____

_____

2. Find out what contact has been made with Mars, and describe any plans for man to travel there.

_____

_____

_____

3. Name three other 20th Century inventions that have had a significant impact on our lives.

_____

_____

_____

4. Do you believe that man has landed on the moon? Support your opinion.

_____

_____

_____

5. If we can travel at the speed of sound, explain why we can't travel at the speed of light.

_____

Adult Reading Comprehension – Book 3

A New Love

While reading the newspaper last evening, I came across a word I didn't know. The article was a review of a famous play called *Les Miserables*. This play is a musical that has been performed all over the world for the last twenty years. Although it is a bit of a depressing story about life during and after the French Revolution, the play manages to include some comic respite. The characters include peasants and a street urchin, among others, and of course there is a love story woven into the plot.

The reviewer said that the lead actor gave a "believable performance portraying the anguish of his situation." I had to look up *anguish*: n. severe mental or physical suffering.

Reading this review, I challenged myself to choose one new word from the newspaper for seven days in a row, learn what each one meant and then write something using them all. I decided to write a poem, but it was a lot harder than I expected, even though I didn't even try to make it rhyme. Here is my poem.

A New Love
Not a <u>fragment</u> remains
Of the <u>angst</u> I felt
When you <u>instigated</u> your departure
From our <u>superficial</u> friendship
For the new love I have <u>encountered</u>
Is <u>immensely</u> more satisfying
And will surely <u>persist</u>.

Questions

1. Find the definitions of five of the words in the author's poem that were selected from the newspaper. Use each one in a sentence to show your understanding.

   _____   _____
   _____   _____
   _____   _____
   _____   _____
   _____   _____

2. In your own words, write the story the poem tells.

   _____
   _____

3. Do what the author did: find seven words in the newspaper that you don't know, learn their definitions from a dictionary. On a separate sheet of paper, use them to write a poem, including a title.

4. Find and read some newspaper reviews of movies or plays. On a separate sheet of paper, write your own review of a play or movie you have seen. Include the title, something about the storyline, the characters and any special costumes or effects.

5. Find and read some newspaper reviews of books. On a separate sheet of paper, write your own review of a book or article you have read.

© 2009 Aber Publishing – Adult Skills   Adult Reading Comprehension – Book 3

The Sinking of the Titanic

The Titanic, built in Ireland, was the largest and most modern of all passenger ships of the time. Its builder claimed that it was unsinkable because of how it was built. It was designed with several watertight compartments. As many as three of them could be flooded and the ship would still stay afloat.

The ship was launched on 11 April 1912 with 1,424 passengers and 800 crew. The destination was New York, which would be a long journey across the Atlantic. On 14 April, as the passengers were enjoying the voyage, the crew received six messages via radio warning them about dangerous icebergs ahead. However, the 'ice-warnings' were not passed on to the captain because the crew believed the ship was incapable of sinking.

Late that evening, the crew spotted an iceberg directly in front of the ship. The officer in charge tried to avoid hitting the iceberg. Unfortunately, the ship not only hit the iceberg, but the ice scraped a huge hole along the side, immediately filling five of the 'watertight' compartments with seawater.

The captain immediately ordered the ship to be evacuated. Due to the shortage of lifeboats, panic and greed, 1,513 people lost their lives that night. The first ship that reached the area 2 hours later found nothing left of the Titanic, but fortunately managed to rescue 700 survivors.

Questions

1. If you were a man on a sinking ship, would you find it hard to give up a place on a lifeboat to a woman or child? Explain your answer.

   _____

   _____

2. List three mistakes that contributed to this tragedy. Which do you think was the biggest mistake? Explain your answer.

   _____

   _____

   _____

3. Circle all the past tense verbs. Choose five of them and give their past, present and future tense.

   _____   _____   _____

   _____   _____   _____

   _____   _____   _____

   _____   _____   _____

   _____   _____   _____

4. Write a short summary of this story.

   _____

   _____

   _____

5. Do some research on icebergs. Write some facts that you learned about them.

   _____

Listen to the Seashells

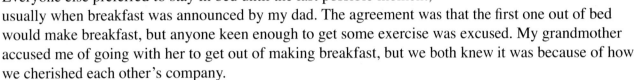

Nana lived in a granny flat behind our house. On our family holidays, we would often go to the seaside. Nana loved to have an early cup of tea and rush out into the fresh sea breezes with me in tow.

Everyone else preferred to stay in bed until the last possible moment, usually when breakfast was announced by my dad. The agreement was that the first one out of bed would make breakfast, but anyone keen enough to get some exercise was excused. My grandmother accused me of going with her to get out of making breakfast, but we both knew it was because of how we cherished each other's company.

There were always lots of shells scattered on the beach. My favourite was the conch, shaped a bit like a spiral that you could put up to your ear and hear the whispering sounds of the sea. Nana said that if you listened assiduously you would receive messages from the people you loved the most.

Nana died last year, and that summer when we went on holiday I got up early the first morning and went down to the beach. As soon as I stepped onto the sand I found a conch shell beside my foot. Tears streamed from my eyes as I put it to my ear, closed my eyes and concentrated on listening to the whispering sounds coming from it.

Questions

1. Write the definition of assiduously, and find two synonyms for it. Use them in sentences to show your understanding of them.

    _____   _____

    _____   _____

    _____   _____

2. Write the main idea of each paragraph.

    _____ _____ _____

3. What does the author mean by this statement: 'with me in tow'? Write two other ways that you can express the same thing.

    _____

    _____

4. Describe a favourite holiday you have had with your family or friends.

    _____

    _____

    _____

5. Write an extra paragraph to finish this story, describing what you think was whispered.

    _____

    _____

    _____

The Art of Tai Chi

There are more than 300 different known styles of martial arts. Tai Chi, an ancient system of physical movement developed in China thousands of years ago, was initially a form of fighting. It was one of the *external* systems of martial arts, emphasising strength, balance, flexibility, speed, physical contact, jumps, kicks and breathing all combined with sound.

The origin of modern Tai Chi is not certain, but there is some evidence that it was developed by a Taoist Priest after observing a white crane preying on a snake. When he attempted to mimic the crane's movements, Tai Chi was created.

Some believe that the basis of modern Tai Chi rests with a doctor. Around 250 AD there was a physician who, besides using medicine to promote health, advocated a system of movement based on wild animals - tigers, deer, bears, apes and birds. He believed that to achieve a long and healthy life, the body needed regular exercise to help with digestion and circulation and that imitating these animals would achieve this.

Through time, Tai Chi has become associated not only with health, but with philosophy as well. It is now known as an *internal* martial arts system, and has evolved into a soft, slow, and gentle form of exercise. Today there are many different types of Tai Chi practised by people of all ages around the world.

Questions

1. What do AD and BC stand for? Do all countries in the world use these initials? Support your answer.

   _____

   _____

2. Arrange to participate in a Tai Chi lesson, or ask a friend to teach you some moves. Write about your experience.

   _____

   _____

   _____

3. Research three other things that the Chinese are known to have invented that spread to other countries. Give their modern names and describe their uses.

   _____

   _____

   _____

4. Explain why the words *internal* and *external* are used to describe different martial arts forms.

   _____

   _____

5. List three forms of *external* martial arts. Compare and contrast them.

   _____

   _____

   _____

Employee of the Month

My older brother Phillip is nearly 30, but unfortunately he has Down Syndrome, a condition which means he has slower than normal mental, motor and language abilities. He is also smaller than average adults. The cause of Down Syndrome is attributed to the presence of an extra chromosome.

In spite of all these challenges, he decided that he was going to apply for a job at the supermarket down the street from our house. I helped him fill out the application and went with him to the interview. As I waited for him I felt incredibly anxious.

He emerged from the interview with the biggest grin on his face. The first thing he did was to hug me. Then he excitedly explained that he was offered a job collecting the trolleys in the carpark.

After six months on the job, his work ethic is impeccable: he has never been late or missed a day of work, has immeasurable patience doing what for most people would be a boring job, and even takes responsibility for retrieving trolleys that have gone 'walk about' down the street.

Last week, the manager surprised Phillip with a salary raise and chose him as the 'Employee of the Month'. During his time working there he has saved every bit of his earnings. One evening we were all dumbfounded to see a new television sitting in the lounge, with a 42" plasma screen. It was a very generous gesture and one that obviously made him feel extremely pleased with himself. I have to admit to feeling enormously guilty about how I spend my salary.

Questions

1. Do some research on Down Syndrome. List some characteristics of people with this condition that were not mentioned in the story.

   _____   _____   _____

   _____   _____   _____

2. What is plasma? Why do they make televisions with it?

   _____

   _____

3. Describe how you think the author felt when his older brother hugged him in public. Support your opinion.

   _____

   _____

4. Discuss with another student what *work ethic* means to each of you. Write your conclusions.

   _____

   _____

5. What do you think the author means by the last sentence in the story?

   _____

   _____

The Killer Tsunami

On 26 December 2004, a 9.0 magnitude earthquake occurred, one of the most powerful earthquakes in decades. It generated a tsunami in the Indian Ocean, and within hours of the earthquake, killer waves radiating from the epicentre slammed into the coastline of 11 Indian Ocean countries. People were carried out to sea, others drowned on beaches or in their homes, and billions of dollars worth of property was demolished from Africa to Thailand.

It is believed to have killed more than 300,000 people in all, and made millions homeless. In addition to the drownings, the lack of food and clean water and the diseases that followed the disaster also contributed to the death toll.

A tsunami is not a single wave but a series of waves. It can be caused by an underwater earthquake, landslide or volcanic eruption. A tsunami starts when a violent movement of the Earth's tectonic plates displaces an enormous amount of water, sending powerful shock waves in every direction.

On the surface, a tsunami can reach speeds up to 800 kms per hour, as fast as a commercial jet. It can cross an entire ocean in a day or less. Once a tsunami reaches shallow water near the coast, its enormous energy can lift giant boulders, flip vehicles, strip entire beaches away, demolish houses and suck people out to sea.

Questions

1. In the context of the story, explain the meaning of the words below. Then use each one in a sentence in a different context than that in the story.

   displaced _____

   _____

   shock _____

   _____

2. After a tsunami is over, list four things that can continue to cause death.

   _____   _____

   _____   _____

3. Do some research to find out about another very destructive tsunami, including the date of its occurrence, its location and cause, and how many lives were lost.

   _____

   _____

   _____

4. What are three natural disasters, not including tsunamis and earthquakes, that can cause a large loss of life?

   _____   _____   _____   _____

5. List all the adjectives in this story.

   _____ _____ _____ _____ _____

   _____ _____ _____ _____ _____

Beware of Black Holes

Airports have always fascinated me, with the planes taking off and landing, the passengers coming and going and the luggage disappearing or appearing through the various 'black holes'. When I decided to apply for a job at the airport it was the luggage handler's position that interested me the most. Two weeks later I started work in my new uniform, shoes and cap. I'm not sure why all the luggage handlers wear caps - they just do.

Once a passenger checks their luggage, it is tagged with a code identifying its destination and sent off on a conveyor belt through the 'black hole'. There are real people inside the hole who sort the luggage by code and ensure it gets put on the appropriate trolley for the right flight. Once the trolleys are loaded they are attached to a tractor that drives them out to the plane.

My training consisted of learning how to sort the luggage, load it on the trolleys, drive the tractor, unload and load the luggage onto the plane. Of course I had to do all this in reverse after a plane landed, in addition to finally setting it onto the correct conveyor belt for the passengers to collect. My favourite jobs are driving the tractor and loading the plane.

When luggage is lost we have to do a trace using the codes on the luggage tags the passengers were given when they checked in. Most of the time the luggage is recovered and sent on to the passengers within 24 hours.

Questions

1. What is the meaning of the astronomy term 'black holes' in the context of this story?

   _____

   _____

2. Think of three reasons why luggage handlers wear caps.

   _____   _____   _____

3. On a separate sheet of paper, list two jobs that you would enjoy having. For each one, give two reasons why you chose it, the approximate annual salary for a starting position, and any special training or experience that would be required.

4. List four jobs not mentioned in the story that people do at airports. Describe the types of uniform/ clothing people in each position would wear.

   _____

   _____

   _____

   _____

5. Select ten words from the story that you don't know how to spell. Write a definition of each one, and practise spelling them until you are successful with all ten.

   _____   _____   _____   _____

   _____   _____   _____   _____

   _____   _____   _____   _____

   _____   _____   _____   _____

Hard Times in Victorian London

Life in Victorian London, during most of the 1800s, was especially
hard. The population growth far exceeded London's ability to
look after the basic needs of its citizens. People lived in horribly
overcrowded slums in the worst conditions imaginable. Thousands,
including young children, worked or begged on the streets for food or money.
Many of the houses, including those of the rich, were infested with bed bugs and rats. Rubbish, including
decomposing animal and vegetable matter not disposed of properly, increased the spread of diseases.
Hygiene and sanitation were very inadequate for everyone - the poor, the middle class and the wealthy
upper class. London's water supply was taken from the Thames River which was also used for dumping
sewage. People became ill from drinking its water and thousands died from cholera.
Eventually scientists learned about bacteria and a link was made between health, sanitation and the
water supply. The water companies started taking their supply from further up the river to avoid the
London sewerage.
An engineer named Joseph Bazalgette was responsible for the building of over 2,100 kms of tunnels and
pipes to divert sewage outside the city. This had an enormous impact on the death rate, and outbreaks of
cholera dropped dramatically.

Questions

1. Why was London described as Victorian?

   _____

2. Define these words and use them in a sentence to show your understanding:

   scarce   _____

                 _____

   inadequate   _____

                 _____

   bacteria   _____

                 _____

   dramatically _____

3. How did taking water from further up the river stop people from getting ill?

   _____

   _____

4. The author mentions three types of classes. On a separate sheet of paper, make a chart with a
   column for each class. Below each class, write 3 ways that people were different.

5. List three reasons why hygiene and sanitation were so bad in Victorian London.

   _____

   _____

© 2009 Aber Publishing – Adult Skills   Adult Reading Comprehension – Book 3

Euthanasia – Where Do You Stand?

Euthanasia, also called mercy killing, is the act of ending the life of a terminally ill person by a medical professional, relative, friend or even the patient themselves. This controversial subject has been debated for hundreds of years. Ancient Greeks were in favour of euthanasia as was Englishman Thomas More (1478-1535) and British philosopher Francis Bacon (1561-1626). There are two types of euthanasia. Voluntary euthanasia is when a person chooses to have their life ended and they express their desire to their doctor. The person is usually terminally ill, in intense pain or enduring unbearable suffering. Many people have a 'living will' in which they describe the situation(s) in which they would like to be put to death, such as living in a permanent vegetative state.

Non-voluntary euthanasia is when a person is unable to make the choice of having their own life ended, such as being in a coma or unable to communicate. In this case the family can make a request to end their loved one's life. But there are not many places in the world where this is legal.

Those who support euthanasia believe that every person has a right to end their life when they choose. Those who oppose it believe that life is precious and under no circumstances should it be taken by anyone for any purpose.

Questions

1. Why is euthanasia also called 'mercy killing'?

   _____

   _____

2. Most people have strong feelings about this topic. Discuss your opinion with someone else and write your conclusions.

   _____

   _____

   _____

3. No matter how you feel, list three pros and three cons about euthanasia that could be used to debate the issue.

   _____   _____   _____

   _____   _____   _____

4. How does the Hippocratic Oath fit in to the argument of euthanasia?

   _____

   _____

5. To show your understanding, explain the difference between voluntary and non-voluntary euthanasia.

   _____

   _____

© 2009 Aber Publishing – Adult Skills   Adult Reading Comprehension – Book 3

I'm Off to Join the Circus

Ever since attending an innovative Cirque de Lumineux performance two years ago when I was 15, I have been imagining that I was part of their troupe. The performers captivated me with their skill, elegance and costumes. Cirque de Lumineux is not a traditional circus with lion tamers, beautiful women riding elephants, scores of clowns emerging from tiny cars and magicians pulling rabbits out of their hats.

Gone is the impression of a shady group of people and an assortment of animals touring the country with one- or two-night stands. Gone are the days of teenagers being enticed to run away from home to join the circus, only to be worked as slaves erecting and dismantling the large tents and bleachers with little return. Gone are the wild animals forced to live in cages, now protected from such abuse by animal rights groups. The performers in Cirque de Lumineaux are well-paid professional gymnasts, dancers, actors and contortionists with exceptional skills. For every two-hour performance, they practise 25 hours. Their trainers and coaches work closely with them, ensuring that all the safety gear is in order.

There is also a group of designers who constantly create new costumes and repair the old ones. This is where I see myself fitting in. I love unusual fabrics and bright colours, and have a flair for design. I have sent a portfolio of my drawings to the producer. That would be the most exciting job I could ever imagine.

Questions

1. What qualities does the writer have that make her a good candidate for the job she wants? What may keep her from getting the job?

   _____

   _____

2. Do you agree that wild animals should not be kept in cages? Explain your answer.

   _____

   _____

   _____

3. Research and list three of the goals of animal rights groups.

   _____

   _____

   _____

4. List 4 words in the story that you are unfamiliar with. Write their definitions from the dictionary and use each in a sentence to show your understanding.

   _____ _____ _____

   _____ _____ _____

   _____ _____ _____

   _____ _____ _____

5. Find two sets of antonyms in the story.

   _____ _____   _____ _____

Women's Role in World War I

Before World War I (1914-1918), jobs for unmarried women were usually limited to domestic service or women's industries such as tailoring, leatherwork and footwear. After marriage most women stayed home and cared for their children and husbands.

For many women, World War I brought the opportunity to work in a variety of new jobs, often taking over the jobs of their husbands, brothers or fathers. Some of these positions had special names: garage attendants were called 'petrol nymphs' and road sweepers were called 'street housemaids'. Women working in munitions and engineering factories were called the 'munitionettes'. It was common for women to be treated as inferior to men, earning lower wages but working longer hours. The Women's Army Auxiliary Corps (WAAC) was set up in 1917, freeing more men to go to war. The Women's Royal Naval Service (WRNS) and the Women's Royal Auxiliary Air Force (WRAAF) were formed soon after.

In 1917 the Women's Land Army (WLA) was formed. This organisation, designed to operate farms whose male workers had gone to war, was especially necessary after food rationing was introduced. During World War I women enjoyed the new independence and comradeship that work offered them even though some jobs were hard and not particularly pleasant. Women came to believe that the view of 'a woman's place is in the home' was changing.

Questions

1. Plan a research study in which you find at least three men and three women in the same or similar jobs. (For example, they might all be managers, real estate sales people, shop assistants or taxi drivers.) Find out what they earn and write a report about your findings.

2. What is food rationing? Why do you think it was introduced in Britain?
   _____
   _____

3. How did World War I outdate this saying: 'a woman's place is in the home'.
   _____
   _____

4. Explain how the war gave women:
   independence   _____
   comradeship   _____
   variety   _____

5. Do you believe that women in the military should be allowed to fight alongside male soldiers? Support your answer.
   _____
   _____
   _____

My Own OE

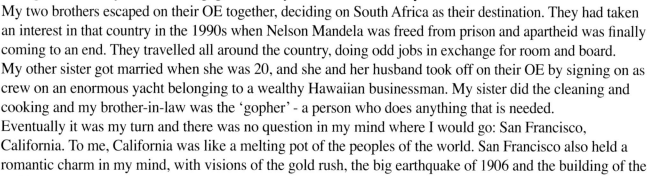

With two sisters and two brothers, all four of them older than me, it seems our family was constantly farewelling one of them on their overseas experiences, or OE as it is generally nicknamed.

First, my sister Sara went to New York where she worked in a hotel restaurant before becoming the assistant catering manager. She has now been gone for four years and is engaged to marry a man from Germany she met there.

My two brothers escaped on their OE together, deciding on South Africa as their destination. They had taken an interest in that country in the 1990s when Nelson Mandela was freed from prison and apartheid was finally coming to an end. They travelled all around the country, doing odd jobs in exchange for room and board.

My other sister got married when she was 20, and she and her husband took off on their OE by signing on as crew on an enormous yacht belonging to a wealthy Hawaiian businessman. My sister did the cleaning and cooking and my brother-in-law was the 'gopher' - a person who does anything that is needed.

Eventually it was my turn and there was no question in my mind where I would go: San Francisco, California. To me, California was like a melting pot of the peoples of the world. San Francisco also held a romantic charm in my mind, with visions of the gold rush, the big earthquake of 1906 and the building of the Golden Gate Bridge.

I wasn't a bit disappointed with my 6-month stay there, working in a fish market on Fisherman's Wharf. On my days off I visited Alcatraz, rode the trolley cars as they trudged up and then coasted down the hills, watched the seals cavort at Pier 39. I was astounded by the number of cruise ships that berthed in the port. It was the most wonderful OE I could have imagined, and I'm saving my money to return some day.

Questions

1. Explain what 'room and board' is.

   _____

2. What is apartheid? Discuss this with your tutor or other students in relation to South Africa. Write down the positive consequences that occurred in South Africa when apartheid was eliminated.

   _____

   _____

   _____

3. List five jobs that you think the writer's brother-in-law did on board the ship.

   _____   _____   _____   _____   _____

4. Explain what 'melting pot' means in the context of this story.

   _____

   _____

5. Choose a destination for your own OE. Explain why you chose it and list what you would like to see if you ever go there.

   _____

   _____

Why Government?

Government, in some form, seems to be necessary to co-ordinate the activity of any large group of people living together in close proximity. Without government, there would be a state of anarchy: the absence of laws, rules and discipline. Some people I know suggest that having no rules to follow would be an ideal way to live. But history shows that in nearly all groups, past and present, a leader soon emerges and a government eventually evolves.

One of the advantages of having a government is that the development and building of services for the citizens can be co-ordinated. Laws and rules allow services to be set up within an orderly structure, which can be funded and operated properly. Some of the many services provided by government are roads, schools, police, emergency services and sewerage and water systems. All nations have some form of government, but not all of them provide quality services. If people grow angry or unhappy with a government's decisions, they can either vote the politicians out or overthrow them. Attempting to overthrow a government is one reason for the many civil wars that have occurred in the world.

Questions

1. List ten services that governments provide to citizens.

    _____   _____
    _____   _____
    _____   _____
    _____   _____
    _____   _____

2. Based on your answers to number 1, rate each service from 1 to 10, with the one you believe is the most important being number 1.

3. Research, compare and contrast three different types of government. Use a separate sheet of paper to write your answer.

4. Do you believe that anarchy would be a good way to live? Support your opinion.

    _____
    _____
    _____
    _____

5. List three advantages and three disadvantages of civil war.
    Advantages   Disadvantages

    _____   _____
    _____   _____
    _____   _____

© 2009 Aber Publishing – Adult Skills   Adult Reading Comprehension – Book 3

Kim's Day

Kim is a student at college in Cardiff. She is studying to be a legal executive. This means she will work in an office with other legal people. Kim is hoping to work on the law with house moves.

Kim remembers the financial problems that started in 2007 that went around the world, so she really understands that moving house or buying your first house can be scary. This is why she does her best to make sure people are very happy with her work. Kim plans to look for work in Cardiff. She likes Cardiff because it is such a cool place for young people. There is so much to do and she can keep in touch with many of her friends when she leaves college. Cardiff is the capital of Wales. Wales has two languages, English and Welsh. Kim's first language is English but she is also learning Welsh. She said ' it is so cool for young people to be able to speak both languages in Wales, after all we are cool Cymru'.

Cymru is the name of Wales in the Welsh language. Kim goes to lectures during the day and then takes her work home to study more. Twice a week she goes out with friends to have fun.

Questions

1   Where does Kim study?

_____

2   Why is Cardiff so special to Kim?

_____

3   How many languages does Wales have?

_____

4   What special role does Cardiff have, as a town in Wales?

_____

_____

© 2009 Aber Publishing – Adult Skills   Adult Reading Comprehension – Book 3